P9-BYC-350

The Perfect Pet

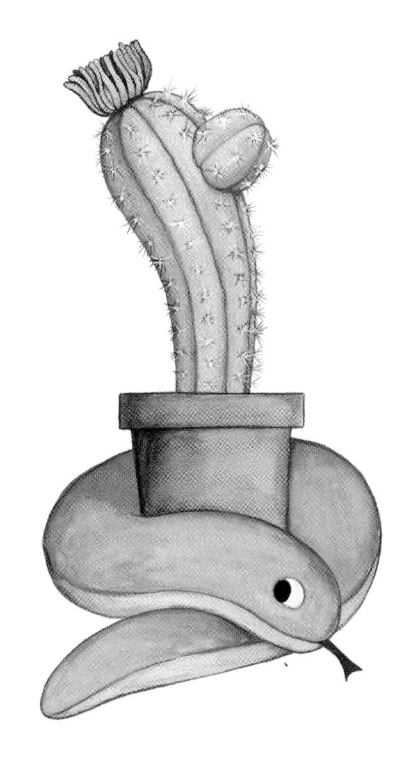

By Margie Palatini · Illustrated by Bruce Whatley

HARPERCOLLINSPUBLISHERS

The Perfect Pet

www.harperchildrens.com

Library of Congress Cataloging-in-Publication Data
Palatini, Margie.
The perfect pet / by Margie Palatini ; illustrated by Bruce Whatley. — 1st ed.
p. cm.
Summary: After Elizabeth's parents do not agree with her various suggestions for the perfect pet, she discovers a solution.
ISBN 0-06-000108-9 — ISBN 0-06-000109-7 (lib. bdg.)
[1. Pets—Fiction. 2. Insects—Fiction.] I. Whatley, Bruce, ill. II. Title.
PZ7.P1755 Pe 2003 2002013384
[E]—dc21 CIP
AC

Typography by Al Cetta
1 2 3 4 5 6 7 8 9 10
❖
First Edition

For my sister, and all her perfect pets—M.P.

To our good friends the Gibbos—B.W.

Elizabeth really, really, *really* wanted a pet. Her parents really, really, *really* did not.

They gave her a plant instead.

Mind you, it was a very good-looking plant, as cactus plants go. And it had quite a prickly sense of humor.

Elizabeth named it Carolyn, which seemed to suit it just fine. It was absolutely no trouble and it was a very good listener.

Snuggling was a bit of a challenge. However, Elizabeth did manage a quick hug now and then.

Elizabeth really, really did like the plant . . . but, she still really, really, *really* wanted a pet.

And she had a plan.

WHALES
BEARS
Pets

THE ELEMENT OF SURPRISE

"So, how about a horse?"

"Huh? What? Who?" said Father.

"Who? What? Huh?" said Mother.

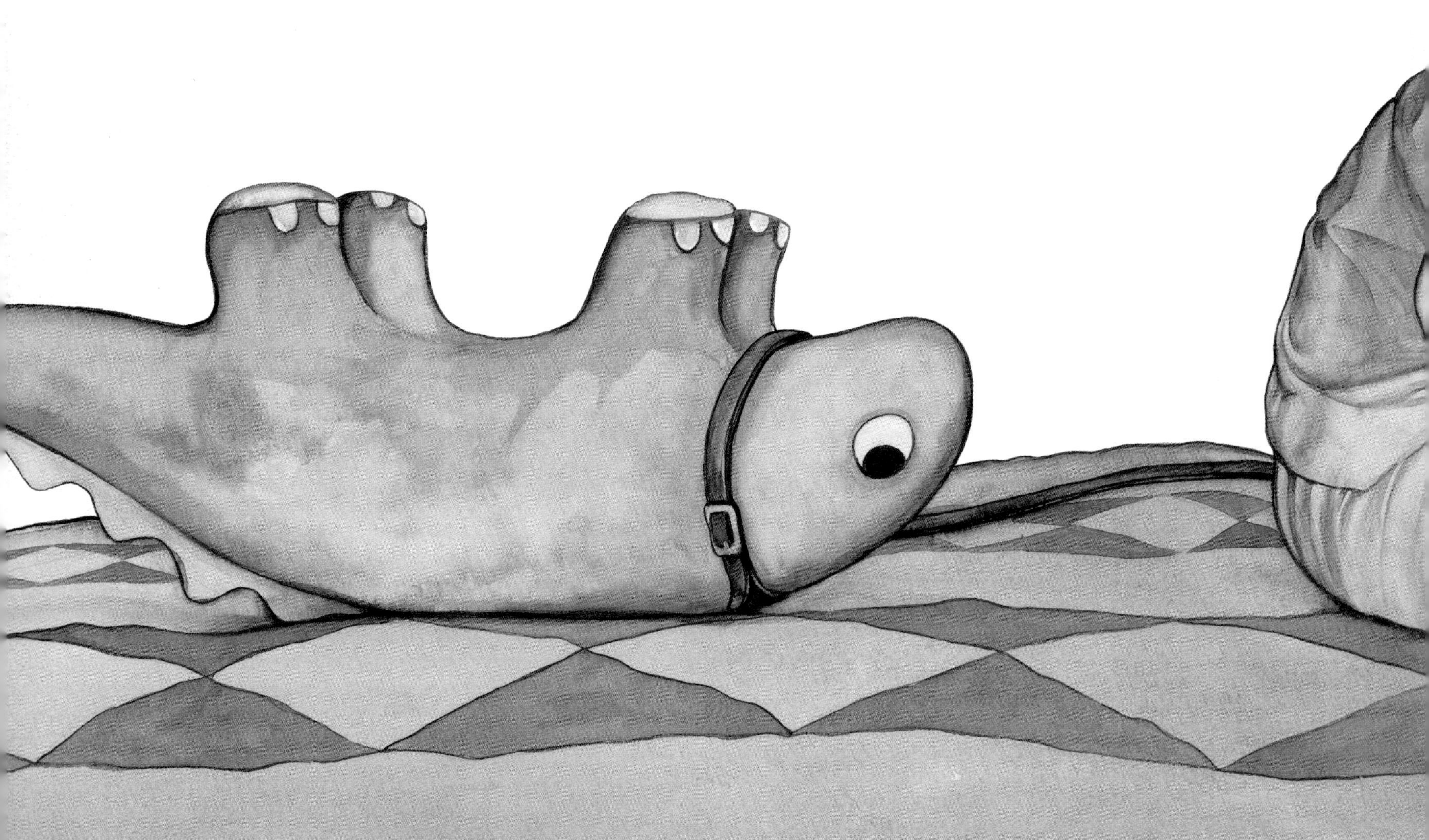

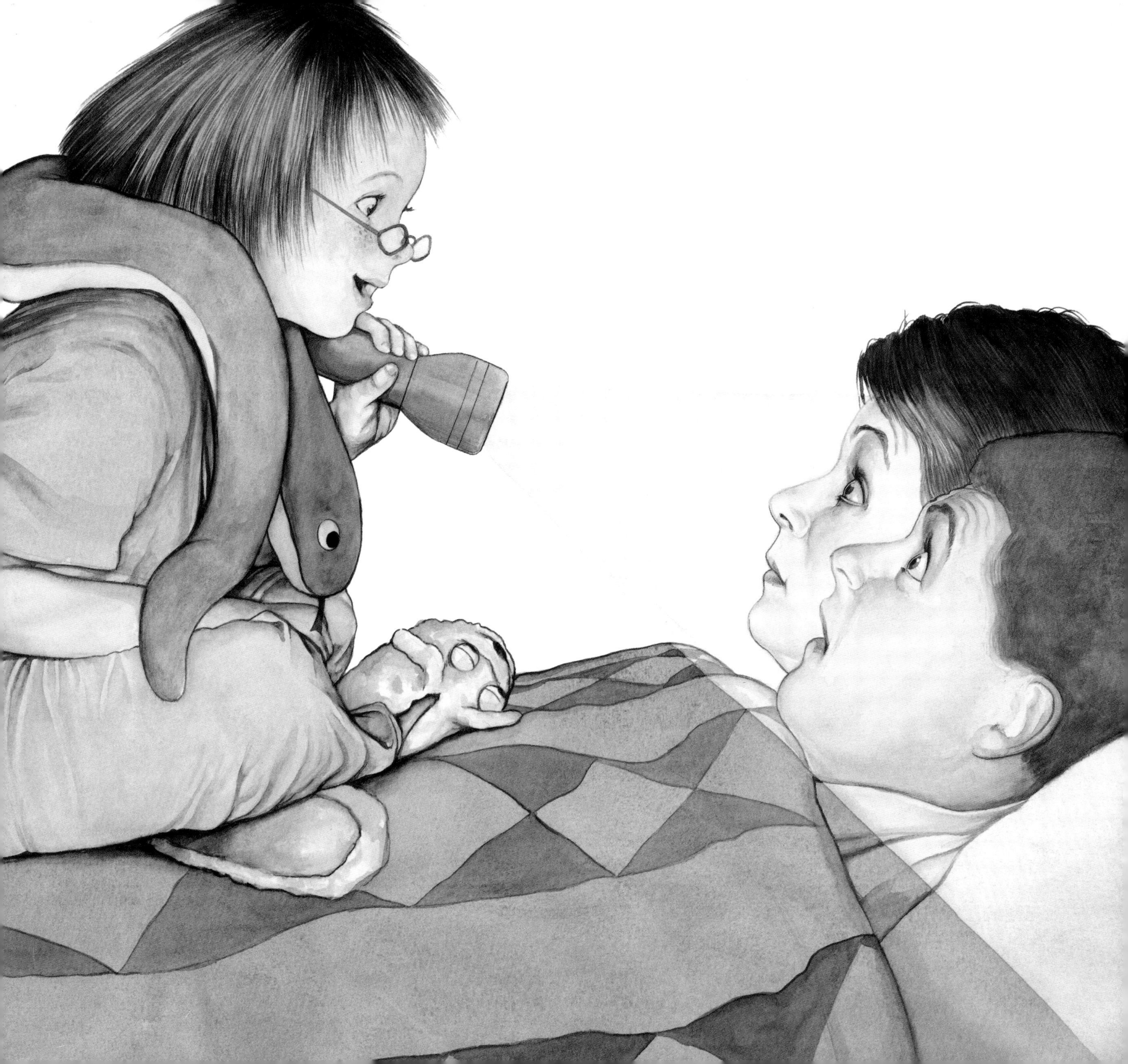

"I could ride it. Give it carrots. Lumps of sugar. A horse would be the perfect pet. Whaddya say?"

Father yawned. "A horse is too big."

Mother sighed. "Our yard is too small."

"Why, it would eat us out of house and home," said Father.

"A horse is not *quite* perfect, dear," said Mother, going back to sleep.

"Not *quite* perfect," said Father sleepily.

Scratch the horse.

CATCH THEM OFF GUARD

"What about a dog?"

"Huh? What? Who?" said Father as he stood in front of the mirror shaving.

"Who? What? Huh?" said Mother, peeking from behind the shower curtain and dripping soapy water.

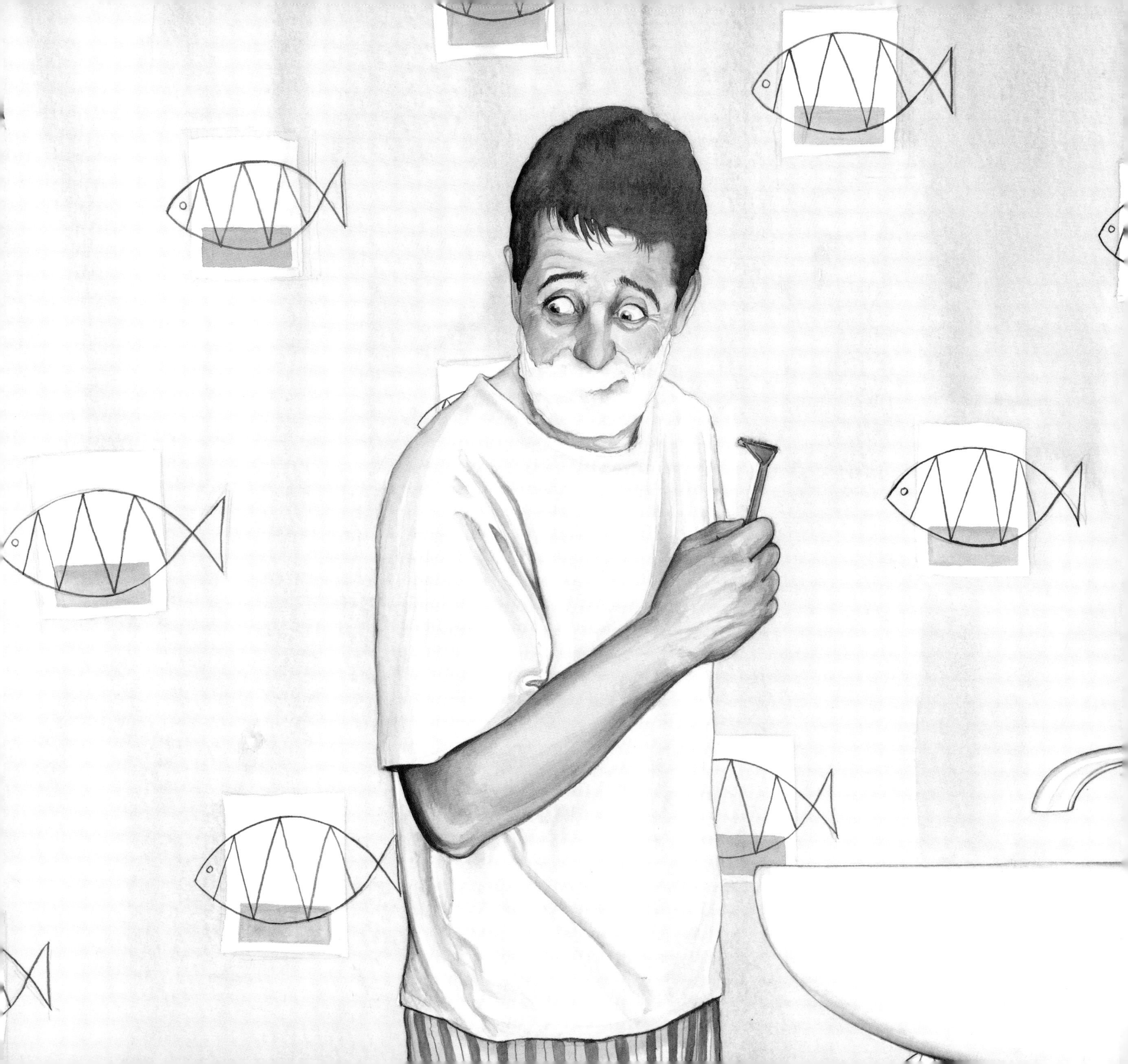

SPORT
POODLE WINS DERBY
BONO
DOG TREATS

"I could take it for walks. Teach it tricks. Feed it treats. Play fetch. A dog would be the perfect pet. Whaddya think?"

Father spit shaving cream. "Dogs bark. They're much too loud."

Mother grabbed a towel. "They jump all over the furniture."

"A dog is not *quite* perfect, Elizabeth," said Father as he shaved.

"Not *quite* perfect," called Mother from the shower.

Forget Fido.

THE FULL STOMACH

Burp.

"You know what would hit the spot right about now?" asked Elizabeth. "I'm thinking . . . a cat."

"Huh? What? Who?" said Father.

"Who? What? Huh?" said Mother.

"A cat could lick the plates. Curl up in my lap. Drink leftover milk. And we'd always know what to do with all that extra string. A cat would be the perfect pet. So . . . how about it?"

Father picked up the newspaper. "Cats scratch."

Mother cleared the table. "Cats shed all over."

"A cat is definitely *not* the perfect pet," said Father.

"Achoo! I'm sneezing already," said Mother.

Cross off kitty.

Mad kitty
runs riot

GO FOR BROKE

"How about a bird?

Bunny?

Turtle?

Fish?

Guinea pig?

Rat?

Any? All?

Take your pick!"

said Elizabeth.

Her parents looked at each other.

"Nope."

"Afraid not."

"Not quite."

"Too fishy."

"Uh-uh."

"Don't even go there."

"What's left?" moaned Elizabeth.

DOUG

Elizabeth was thinking she would never ever find the really, really, *really* perfect pet, when . . . what do you know? She really, really did.

In fact, she almost stepped on it.

Right there on her rug. A bug.

Elizabeth picked him up.

She held him in her hand. Looked him in the eyes.

He wasn't too big. He most definitely was not too loud.

He couldn't jump on the furniture. Didn't scratch. Didn't shed. And how much food could he possibly eat?

He was the perfect pet.

Carolyn totally agreed.

SAFETY

SNUG

Doug moved right in to the lovely house in the corner of Elizabeth's room. It had everything a bug could possibly want and more. Including his very own cactus plant, as Carolyn was only a hop, skip, and jump away. He truly enjoyed sunning himself in her sand.

Of course, Elizabeth provided him with enough crumbs to satisfy any growing bug's appetite.

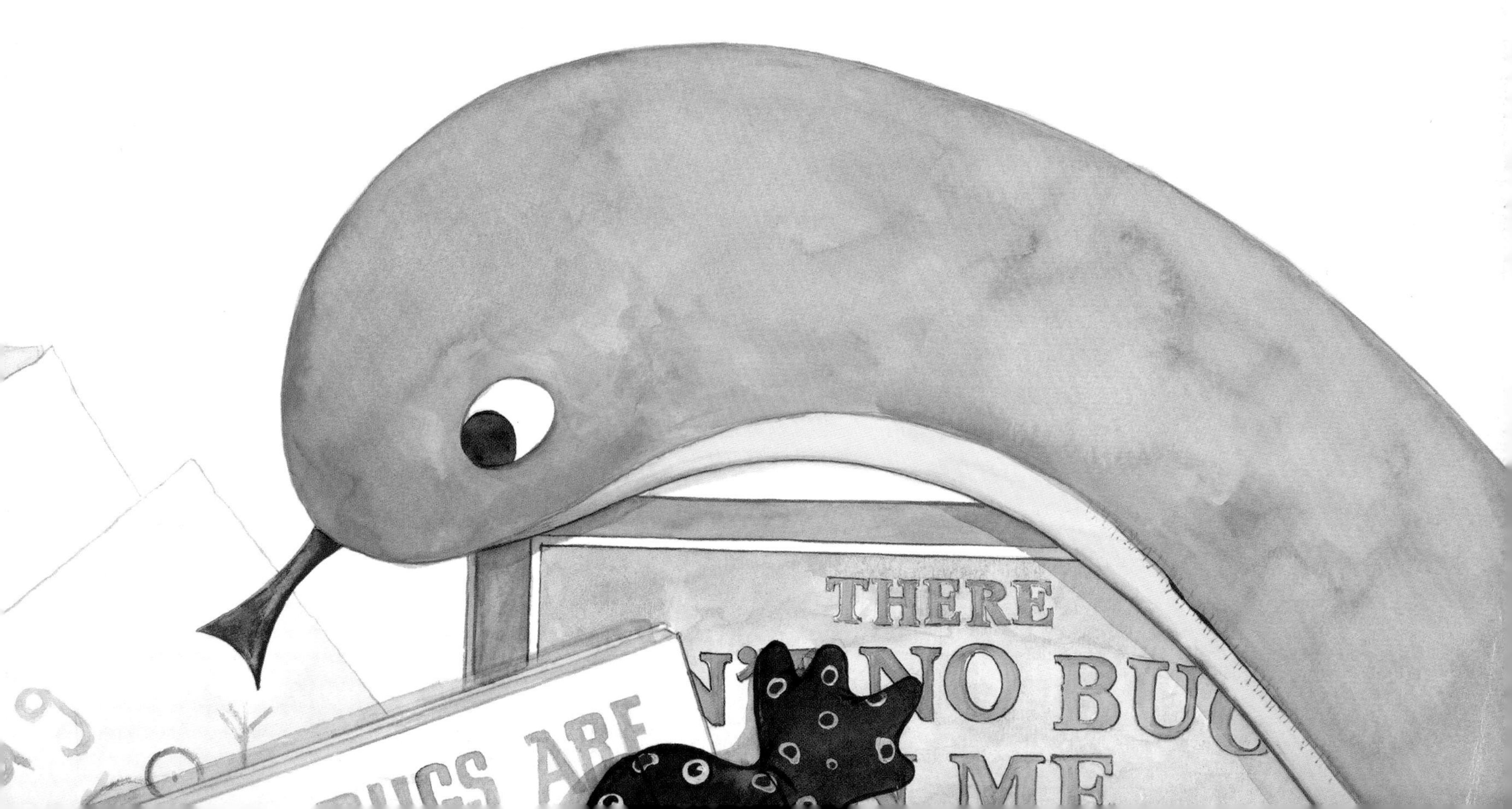

As expected, their relationship was a *tad* different than the usual.

Doug could not give Elizabeth a pony ride. She could not take him for a walk.

He could not catch a ball or fetch, no matter how many times they practiced.

And try as he might, Doug just couldn't get the hang of playing with string.

But he was very helpful with homework. (He always knew where to put a decimal or a period.)

And he loved snuggling up with Elizabeth each night for a story.

What more could you ask? He was perfect.

UNSNUGGED

With all those crumbs and plenty of sun, Doug grew by leaps and bounds. He was one big, healthy bug . . . and then some.

The only trouble really, really, *really* came one Saturday morning, many weeks later. Elizabeth's mother came into her bedroom to get the laundry and . . .

"THERE'S A BUG IN THAT BED!" she screamed.

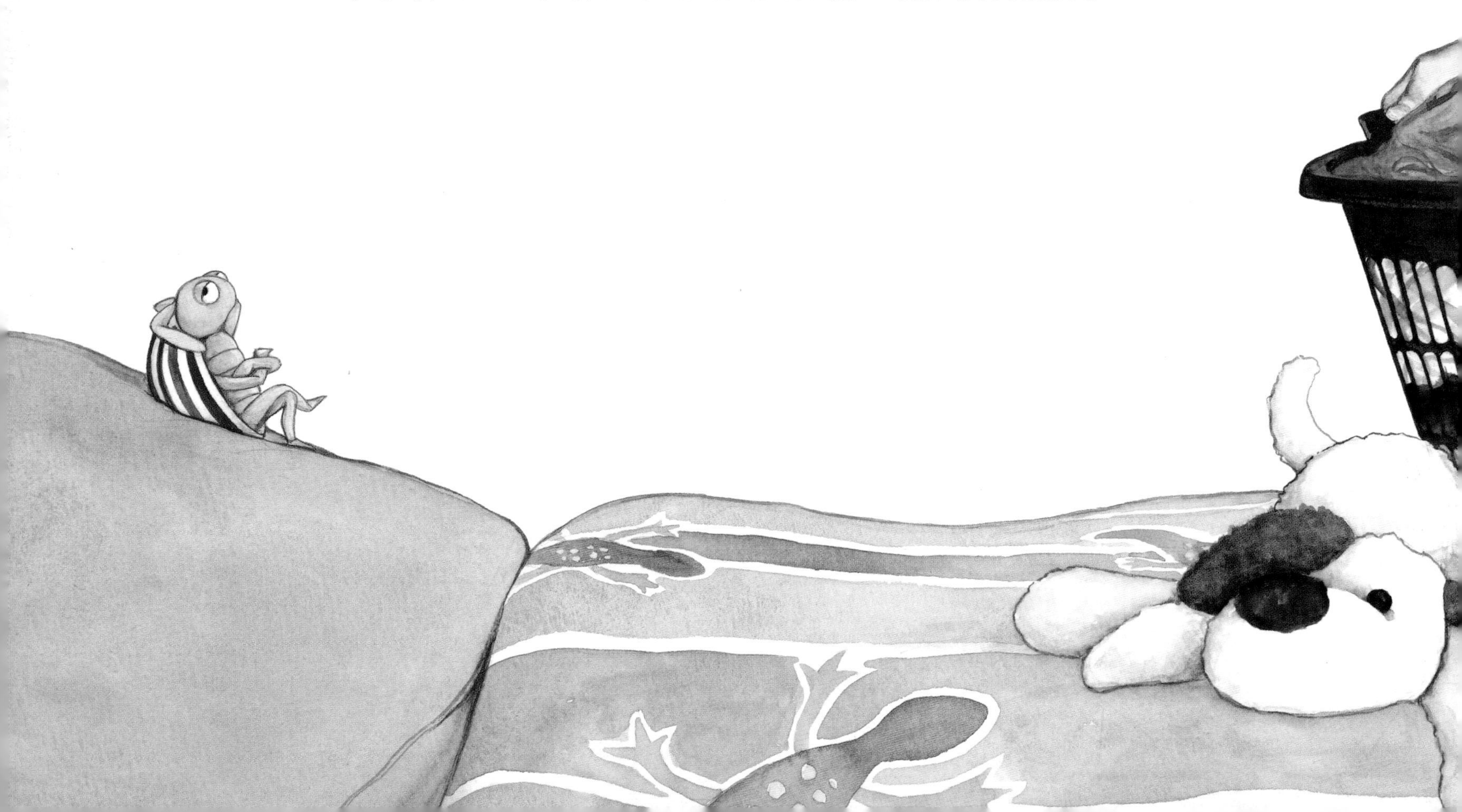

"A bug!" shouted Father, ready to swat.

"That's Doug," said Elizabeth very protectively. "He's my pet."

Her parents looked at each other. "Pet?"

"Pet," said Elizabeth. "Just like you wanted. He's not big like a horse. He isn't loud like a dog. He doesn't jump on furniture, scratch, or shed. And he hardly eats a thing."

"But, a *bug?*" asked Father.

"A *bug?*" repeated Mother.

"*Doug,*" said Elizabeth. "And he's perfect."

ONE BIG HAPPY FAMILY

"Think we should have said 'yes' to the dog?" whispered Father to Mother.

Mother shrugged. "I don't know. We have more room on the couch with the bug."

Elizabeth smiled and tossed Doug a piece of popcorn.